Dear Parents and Educators,

Welcome to Penguin Young Readers! As parents and educators, you know that each child develops at his or her own pace—in terms of speech, critical thinking, and, of course, reading. Penguin Young Readers recognizes this fact. As a result, each Penguin Young Readers book is assigned a traditional easy-to-read level (1–4) as well as a Guided Reading Level (A–P). Both of these systems will help you choose the right book for your child. Please refer to the back of each book for specific leveling information. Penguin Young Readers features esteemed authors and illustrators, stories about favorite characters, fascinating nonfiction, and more!

Tiny the Birthday Dog

LEVEL 1

GUIDED READING LEVEL **D**

This book is perfect for an **Emergent Reader** who:
• can read in a left-to-right and top-to-bottom progression;
• can recognize some beginning and ending letter sounds;
• can use picture clues to help tell the story; and
• can understand the basic plot and sequence of simple stories.

Here are some **activities** you can do during and after reading this book:
• Characters' Feelings: Pretend you are Tiny. How would you feel if you didn't know what was happening inside the house? What would you do outside while you waited?
• Creative Writing: Pretend you are throwing a birthday party for Tiny. Create an invitation. Where will the party be held? What is the date and time? Come up with a theme for the party. Make a list of games that you will play. And don't forget to write a list of whom you want to invite!

Remember, sharing the love of reading with a child is the best gift you can give!

—Bonnie Bader, EdM
  Penguin Young Readers program

*Penguin Young Readers are leveled by independent reviewers applying the standards developed by Irene Fountas and Gay Su Pinnell in *Matching Books to Readers: Using Leveled Books in Guided Reading*, Heinemann, 1999.

For Rich, with many thanks. —CM

To Jesus Christ, the One who lives in me
and creates through me . . . to Him be all the glory.
—RD

Penguin Young Readers
Published by the Penguin Group
Penguin Group (USA) Inc., 375 Hudson Street, New York, New York 10014, USA
Penguin Group (Canada), 90 Eglinton Avenue East, Suite 700, Toronto, Ontario M4P 2Y3, Canada
(a division of Pearson Penguin Canada Inc.)
Penguin Books Ltd, 80 Strand, London WC2R 0RL, England
Penguin Ireland, 25 St Stephen's Green, Dublin 2, Ireland (a division of Penguin Books Ltd)
Penguin Group (Australia), 707 Collins Street, Melbourne, Victoria 3008, Australia
(a division of Pearson Australia Group Pty Ltd)
Penguin Books India Pvt Ltd, 11 Community Centre, Panchsheel Park, New Delhi–110 017, India
Penguin Group (NZ), 67 Apollo Drive, Rosedale, Auckland 0632, New Zealand
(a division of Pearson New Zealand Ltd)
Penguin Books (South Africa), Rosebank Office Park, 181 Jan Smuts Avenue,
Parktown North 2193, South Africa
Penguin China, B7 Jaiming Center, 27 East Third Ring Road North, Chaoyang District,
Beijing 100020, China

Penguin Books Ltd, Registered Offices: 80 Strand, London WC2R 0RL, England

Text copyright © 2013 by Cari Meister. Illustrations copyright © 2013 by Richard D. Davis.
All rights reserved. Published by Penguin Young Readers, a division of Penguin Young Readers Group,
345 Hudson Street, New York, New York 10014. Manufactured in China.

LIBRARY OF CONGRESS CATALOGING-IN-PUBLICATION DATA
Meister, Cari.
Tiny the birthday dog / by Cari Meister ; illustrated by Rich Davis.
p. cm. — (Tiny)
Summary: "Eliot prepares a birthday party for his canine friend, a big dog named Tiny"— Provided
by publisher.
ISBN 978-0-670-01413-2 (hardcover) — ISBN 978-0-448-46478-7 (pbk.) [1. Birthdays—Fiction
2. Parties—Fiction. 3. Dogs—Fiction.] I. Davis, Rich, 1958- ill. II. Title.
PZ7.M515916Tgt 2013 [E]—dc23 2012027542

ISBN 978-0-670-01413-2 (hc)   10 9 8 7 6 5 4 3 2 1
ISBN 978-0-448-46478-7 (pbk)   10 9 8 7 6 5 4 3 2 1

ALWAYS LEARNING   PEARSON

TINY the Birthday Dog

by Cari Meister
illustrated by Rich Davis

Penguin Young Readers
An Imprint of Penguin Group (USA) Inc.

This is Tiny.

Today is his birthday.

I will plan a party.

Shh! It is a surprise!

I need to get ready.

I tell Tiny to play outside.

Go, Tiny!

Tiny does not want to go.

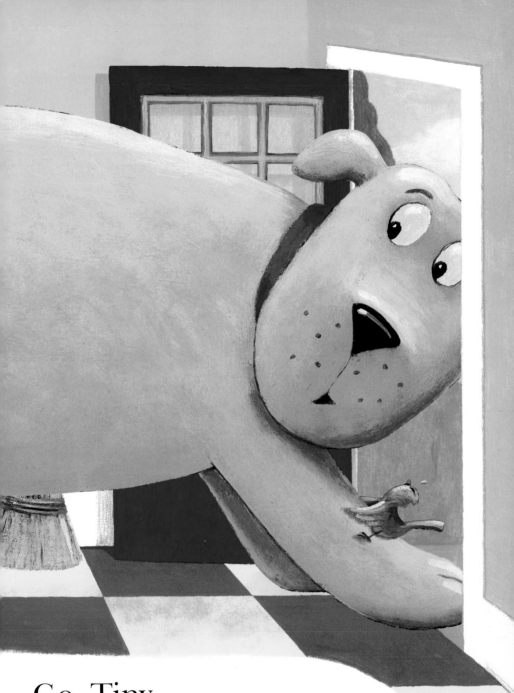

Go, Tiny.

Go outside.

Tiny sits by the door.

He waits.

I blow up balloons.

Pop!

Tiny barks.

Tiny barks and barks.

He wants to come in.

Sorry, Tiny.

You have to wait outside.

I make a cake.

Tiny taps on the door.

Tiny has a ball.

Not now, Tiny.

I have work to do.

I get Tiny's present.

I need a lot of paper.

I need a lot of tape.

There! I hope he likes it.

Tiny looks in the window.

No peeking, Tiny!

We put on party hats.

26

We put up a banner.

I get the cake.

There! All set!

Okay, Tiny.

Now you can come in.

Surprise!

Happy birthday, Tiny!